S0-CYH-977

JUST IN-BETWEEN

(Original title: Leo the Lioness)

Constance C. Greene

SCHOLASTIC BOOK SERVICES

New York Toronto London Auckland Sydney Tokyo

Cover illustration by Amy Rowen

ISBN 0-590-32016-5

12 11 10 9 8 7 6 5 4 3 2 1   11   1 2 3 4 5 6/8

Printed in the U.S.A.   06

To my father

1.

"IBB, you are a slob," my sister Nina said.

I didn't answer her. It was not the kind of remark that required an answer.

She has called me worse things.

She thinks she's so much just because, all of a sudden, boys call her up on the telephone. Not just one boy but two.

Why not? She was fifteen last May. It is about time. She is a Gemini. That is the third sign of the zodiac and it means twins. She also has a split personality. Which means she is either up or down but never in between.

That is true. If she is in an up mood, she is sweet and smiling and pleasant. If she is in a down one, beware! That is all I can say. Beware.

She had been in a down mood for quite a few days until these boys called her. One she knew because he was in her French class. The other, named Tiger Jones, if you can bear it, had seen her at the beach and found out her name from a friend of a friend. Any boy who actually calls himself Tiger with a straight face I could not give the time of day to, but we are different, Nina and I.

Anyway, I think she had about given up hope. About boys calling her, that is. But then my mother broke down and bought her a bikini. She says it's a bikini but it's the biggest bikini I've ever seen.

You can hardly even see her belly button.

I don't call that much of a bikini, but people believe what they want to believe. The capacity for self-deception in people is really amazing. It is especially strong in Geminians, or whatever you call them.

She also bought some stuff to streak her hair with. Her hair is quite nice, sort of a dirty blond, like mine, but she wanted to streak it. All the kids she knows are streaking theirs.

Not only that, but she said she had to buy a bigger bra. She doesn't look any different to me. She was about to send away to one of those courses they advertise in magazines, showing a woman BEFORE, who looks O.K. to me, then she takes this course and AFTER she looks like a sex symbol. Those are not my words. That's what they call women with big chests, sex symbols.

My mother said the AFTER picture made the woman look like a nursing mother.

My mother can be quite earthy at times.

I don't understand what all this fuss about bosoms is. I know kids in my class who stuff their bras with Kleenex so they'll look like sex symbols. If they only knew. The Kleenex looks all lumpy and bumpy and wouldn't fool a baby.

I myself do not have a figure. I probably never will. I have grown almost three inches in the last year and I will not be fourteen until August. I am a Leo. That is the best sign of the zodiac. Leo the Lion is king of the beasts and people born under this sign are very strong, forceful, steadfast, and practically everything good.

"Be glad you are tall," my mother said. "It is far better to be tall than to be short. You will notice that all fashion models are tall and slender. Just remember to stand up straight; never hunch your shoulders and pretend you are shorter. Stand straight and throw your shoulders back and hold your head up. I envy you."

It is interesting to note that when my mother stands as tall as she is able, she comes to my ear. She wears a size six shoe. I wear an eight. My hands are also large. I would say "enormous" but I have been accused of exaggerating by too many people, so I will stick to "large." I drop things when I am nervous and even when I'm not. I stumble over chairs and couches and stuff like that. Even when I'm careful I do.

The last time my grandmother came to visit, I slopped tea in the saucer and on her and spilled a whole plate of cookies in her lap. She said, "Don't worry, Tibb, it'll wash right out," and when I went to get a sponge to clean the mess up, I heard her say, "She is just like a young colt."

She didn't mean to hurt my feelings but I went out to the kitchen and cried anyway. It is sort of interesting to watch yourself in the mirror when you cry. People are so ugly when they cry. I am particularly so. My nose gets red and swells up and my face gets even more spotted and my eyelids puff up. I am hideous.

I have always wanted a colt of my own. My father said he would buy me one if we ever moved to a place where we had room.

That'll be never.

If you can't own a colt, I've decided, you might as well be like one.

2.

NINA and I fight a lot. We didn't use to. As a matter of fact, we were good friends when we were little. We played secret games and had secret signs that nobody else understood. I used to let her come into my bed when there was a thunderstorm. We are only a little more than a year apart and my mother used to dress us alike. People mistook us for twins, which we sometimes pretended to be. Now when I remind Nina of this, she makes a gagging sound and says, "You and me! Twins! You must be out of your mind."

She has a rather unfortunate personality at times. I myself find that persons born under the sign of Gemini are a little tough to take.

I have a friend named Jennifer. She is a Pisces and she is also getting tough to take. She and I were both going to be vets when we grew up. I would still like to be one but Jen gets mad when I talk about the plans we made long ago.

She has even changed her name. That will give you some idea of the phoniness that besets people when they are Gemini or Pisces and also when they hit the age of puberty. Or it hits them. Jen is six months older than I am, so she is almost closer in age to Nina.

Anyway, last time I called her on the telephone, I asked to speak to Jen.

"Oh, we don't have anyone here by that name," her mother said. I knew it was her mother because I've been calling that house since I was six years old.

"Isn't this TOwnsend 8–3560?" I asked, just to be sure.

"Indeed it is, but we do not have a 'Jen' here. We do, however, have a 'Niffy.' "

"A Niffy?" I said. I thought maybe it was some kind of a new cereal. "This is Tibb, Mrs. Stone," I said.

"Oh, Tibb, how are you? Jen has decided she will not answer to 'Jen' any more. We are instructed to call her 'Niffy' from now on. I am finding it rather difficult to break a habit of fourteen years, but I am trying."

"Oh," I said. "Well, is Niffy there then?" I felt like a fool.

"Just a minute," she said. "Niffy, your friend Tibb is on the phone."

"Hello," the voice said.

"Jen?"

"No, this is Niffy." It didn't even sound like her.

"You've got to be kidding," I said. "How come you've changed your name?"

"You wouldn't understand," Jen said. "You are too young."

"Oh, splat," I said. "You are getting to be a pain in the neck. What's come over you?"

"It just so happens," she said, "that I have a date tonight."

"Who with? An orangutan?"

"It just so happens it's with a boy from out of town," Jen said.

"I didn't think it was anybody you knew," I said. "You have to be careful of blind dates. You might get stuck with someone who smokes pot or one of those."

"It is not a blind date." I could practically see Jen sticking out her lip.

"Who is it then?"

"It is this son of a friend of my mother's. He is seventeen and is going to college in the fall," she said. "And I have met him so it is not a blind date, smarty pants." She sounded like the old Jen for a minute.

"All I can say is, if a kid who's about to go to college takes out a girl who's fourteen years old, there must be something wrong with him. When'd you meet him, when you were six months old and he was a big boy of three? Did you two sport around together in your diapers?"

I can be very nasty at times. I have a cutting tongue. But not without provocation. This is not characteristic of Leos as a rule.

"You'll have to excuse me," Jen said. "I'm drawing a bath."

She shouldn't lay herself open like that.

"Oh, I didn't know you had taken up art," I said and hung up fast, beating her to it.

I went to look at myself in the mirror. I find that I do this frequently when I am feeling an excess of emotion. Like I said, I watched myself crying and now I watched myself being mad.

I am quite ugly. My ears stick out a little and my nose is too big for my face. My complexion has its ups and downs, just like Nina's disposition. Today it is in a down period.

If they were casting Cinderalla, I could play one of the stepsisters.

I feel like a stepsister.

3.

"TIBB, you are the best person who ever happened to me," John said. It was right after I'd finished reading him a story. He likes to be read to because he likes to hear the words aloud rather than in his head. Also because it is easier. John is not too hot a reader.

He is my brother. He is seven and has a very good sense of humor. He laughs at all my jokes. John still sucks his thumb but only when he is very tired. He is a joyous child. That is the best word I can think of to describe him. Joyous. He looks like one of those stick-figure drawings you sometimes see. His arms and legs are like pipe-stems and he has this marvelous head which is a little too big for the rest of him. He will grow into it. His hair is very blond in the summer, which it is now, but in the winter it is dirty blond, like Nina's and mine.

John is very pleased with life. Every day is like a whole new adventure to him. He wears an enormous hat, an old straw beach hat of my mother's, and under that hat he looks like an elf.

John is a Taurus. Next to Leo, Taurus is the strongest sign of the zodiac. My mother is also a Taurus. John was born on April 28, the day after her birthday. She said at first she thought this was a nice idea until John started agitating about his birthday six months before.

"We have to start thinking about the party and the presents," he would say around the middle of October.

"Good heavens," my mother said, "it's not for months yet. It seems as if we just had a birthday. Don't make me age so fast. We still have Christmas to get through."

"It's not too early to start thinking about my birthday," John said. He can be very stubborn at times. This is an outstanding characteristic of people born under the sign of Taurus. The Bull, you know.

"I would like a bird's nest and an aquarium and a flashlight. That is all."

"Make a list," my mother said.

I helped him with the spelling and he made a

list. My mother put it somewhere and then she couldn't remember where, which was all right because John changed his mind several times before he settled on what he really wanted.

Which was an ant farm and a Kennedy half dollar.

He got both.

4.

MY father said, "What's in the stars today, Lioness?" He calls me that because, as I said, I am a Leo. I do not let him leave for work in the morning without reading him his horoscope which comes in the morning paper. We also get an evening paper which has another horoscope for the following day, so that way we have the whole twenty-four-hour period covered.

"Just a minute, Dad," I said. I have to read my own first. "Look away from your own problems," it said, "and listen to those of your friends."

Well. My own problems are so many and so varied that I do not know if it is possible for me to look away from them. Most of my friends have similar problems, which in itself proves to be a problem. I can't see the forest for the trees, as the old saying goes. I think it was Shakespeare but I'm not absolutely certain.

Most of my friends are worried because they are too tall or too short or too fat or too thin or they have bad breath or perspiration odor or one of those. There is that to be said for television; when you watch those commercials over and over it makes you much more conscious of all the things that could go wrong. I never realized getting yourself to smell sweet and be reasonably presentable was such an enormous undertaking until those commercials pointed out to me all the things that could go wrong. It is a very depressing thing to see those commercials one after another. You would have to have an enormous amount of self-confidence not to get depressed.

O.K. So I press on to my father's horoscope.

"Your ideas should be kept for a better time and place," I read to him. "Turn to young people for a lift."

"For a lift?" my father said. "Good gravy! Young people are going to drive me either to the loony bin or to the poorhouse. One way or the other, they're going to get me. I'm going to write to that horoscope expert and demand my money back."

My father is a Scorpio. He is musical and plays the harmonica very well. He also sings, but only old songs like "Deep Purple" or "Chattanooga Choo-Choo." And he says *our* songs are dumb.

He is very clever with his hands and has wallpapered the hall and the dining room. He does a better job than a professional, which he will tell you himself. My mother is the painter in the family. She paints the woodwork and the window sashes, only she is not as careful as he is and he goes around and inspects her work after she is finished and points out spots she missed. All of which drives her crazy.

He also built a bookcase in the hall and we almost never have to have a plumber in because he is a first-class operator with the plunger and stuff like that. When John was small he used to throw quite a few articles down the toilet. It saves a lot of money to have someone in the house who knows how to put in new washers and fix stoves, which he also does.

John is very proud of using my father's tools and is constantly making off with hammers and screwdrivers so that when Dad wants to use them, they are gone. Then my father hollers and tells John to go and find them, which he usually does, only by that time they are so rusty, due to the fact they have been rained on quite a lot, that they are no longer any good.

John has his own set of tools, small ones, but he likes my father's big ones better.

That figures.

5.

"TIBB, really!" my mother said. "I've asked you three times to get the groceries out of the car."

"I didn't hear you the last two," I said. "How come Nina-concertina can't manage it?"

"I asked you."

I really like my mother, although she and I aren't hitting it off too well lately. We used to get on very well together and once in a while would have a conversation that, if anyone overheard it, they would probably think we were friends and not relatives at all. But recently we seem to snap at each other quite a bit. I have heard about the change of life but I don't think she is going through that because she is only thirty-eight. A well-preserved thirty-eight, as she would be only too glad to tell you.

So I decided I would go and get the groceries out of the car and not say anything more about Nina, who goofs off every time she hears the car come into the driveway. She runs into the bathroom and locks the door and turns the shower on. My mother, whom I consider a reasonably bright person, falls for it every time.

I took the watermelon out of the back seat and also the sack of potatoes. I tried balancing the potatoes on my head but they were too lumpy so they smashed to the pavement.

My mother watched from the front door.

"They're only potatoes," I said. "I wouldn't have tried it if they'd been eggs."

"I'd hate to put any money on it," my mother said.

"Tibb," she said while we were putting the groceries away, "you're getting awfully leggy."

"Yeah," I said. "I'm getting pretty army, too."

That is true. My arms seem to be getting longer and longer. I am really a little worried about them. Suppose they keep on growing until they hit the ground? What then? If I were friends with Nina and Jen, I would ask them if they thought my arms were getting unnaturally long. But I am not friends with them and my other good friends have gone away for the summer. I have this friend — Susan Friend is her name (would you believe it?) — and her father and mother took her to Europe this summer. She does not speak a foreign language. She has taken French for about a billion years but she can hardly ask for a pencil or say *Bonjour*, so you just know she won't be able to communicate. Anyway, she was practically in a catatonic state about the whole thing. Catatonic is one of the words I have just discovered and use with some frequency, mostly because it drives Nina up the wall. She pretends that she knows what it means and that it is not worthy of her attention, but I know when I say somebody is in a catatonic state, she grits her teeth and wants to smack me. For some reason, this gives me a great deal of pleasure.

I got a post card from Susan the other day from Rome. She wrote: "There are a lot of cathedrals here. Also there seem to be a great many Italians. See ya, Sue."

I read it a couple of times. Susan is the kind of person that, when she says something like that, you don't know whether she is putting you on or whether she actually finds it strange that there are a lot of Italians in Rome. We have been friends for ages but she is not all that bright. I find when you have friends for a long time, you find other qualities in them which make up for lack of brains. Susan is a Virgo, having been born the twenty-third of August, which means she just missed being a Leo. I would never say it to her, of course, but I secretly feel that this one day might have made all the difference.

"Mom," I said when we finally finished our job and she was making up a list of all the things she'd forgotten at the store, "I think I'm finally there."

"Where?" she asked.

"Where the brook and the river meet," I said.

About two years ago, when Nina first became difficult, my mother said that Nina was where the brook and the river met and we would all have to be patient. At that time I was not sure what she meant but now I have figured it out. At that time, also, I hoped that I would never get to that spot because I might get washed away. I thought that was pretty good, but I kept it to myself. Sometimes it is best to keep your witticisms to yourself until the appropriate time comes.

This was the appropriate time.

"Oh, dear," my mother said.

"Yes," I said, "I fear that I am there. I just hope I don't get washed away."

My mother looked at me.

"Is that original?" she asked.

"Yes," I said. "I thought of it just now." I

added that white lie because it made the story better.

"You won't," she said, patting my cheek. "You won't. It may be quite a swim, but I have faith in you."

"So do I," John said from under his hat. He goes to this Y day camp where they teach him to make lanyards. He has so many lanyards around his neck he can hardly walk.

For some reason I felt quite happy.

6.

"HOW was your date?" I asked Jen. She had come over to return a lasagna pan her mother had borrowed from mine. It was the first time I'd seen her since she'd changed her name. I avoided calling her anything.

Jen flicked her eyelashes at me. She had forgotten that I know that when she flicks her eyelashes, she is getting ready to tell a lie. Not a white lie, a whopper.

"Gawd, he was something," she said. Jen and Nina and others in their crowd have taken to saying "Gawd," which for some reason they think is not as profane as saying "God." It is all part of the pattern of self-deception I was talking about.

"How do you mean, 'something'?"

"Well, he had a black beard and sideburns and everything," Jen said. "My mother practically had a cow when she saw him. If he hadn't been a son of a friend, she would've never allowed me to go out with him."

That is probably true. I have noticed that if your mother knows a boy's mother and they happen to be old school chums, she will let her daughter go out with him even if he should prove to be an incipient rapist. This is horribly strange but true.

"He's going to go out for the wrestling team when he gets to college and he has these fantastic muscles and all."

"Wow," I said.

"Don't be sarcastic," Jen said.

"Who's being sarcastic? All I said was 'Wow.' "

"It's the way you said it."

"What'd you tell him your name was?" I couldn't resist asking.

"I told him my name was Jennifer but my friends call me Niffy. He thought it was cute."

"He sounds like a winner," I said. "Did he ask you to go out again?"

Jen flicked her eyelashes like mad. "He said when he gets up to college and gets settled and all, he'll write and arrange a date. Maybe a prom weekend."

"Does he know how old you are?" I asked.

"I told him I was almost sixteen," Jen said. "I hope he doesn't check with his mother."

"Mothers never remember how old other people's kids are," I said. It has been my experience that this is true. They always think other people's kids are a lot younger than they really are.

"I can just see your mother's face when you ask her if you can go to a college weekend," I said. "What'll you do if he tries to make out with you?"

"I'll cross that bridge when I come to it," Jen said airily. "I can handle boys. I just finished reading an article on how to stop boys who get fresh and still make them like you."

"How do you do that?" I asked.

"You remain good-humored," Jen said and I could see she had memorized the article. "You sort of slither away but always keep a smile on your face and toss off a little joke so he won't get angry at being rejected."

"You better keep a stockpile of little jokes on hand," I said. "I understand boys are out for just one thing. S-E-X."

I had heard enough conversations among older girls, not to mention my contemporaries, to know that very few boys, and they have to be queer, are content just to hold hands any more. Or even with kissing. They are always pawing girls and sticking their tongues in their mouths and disgusting things like that. It occurred to me that boys my own age have to overcome quite a few inhibitions of their own. You can't tell me that all boys, regardless, want to leap on top of a girl and make out when they're just out for a movie or a soda or something. That's ridiculous. Anyway, not all boys know what to do. They don't know all that much about sex. And people say the sex urge is the strongest drive in man. Well, maybe. I know it's supposed to be practically overpowering. I still give boys credit for some kind of discrimination so that they don't want to have sex with everything in skirts. That doesn't sound likely. Most of my friends wear pants more frequently than they wear skirts, but you know what I mean. In any event, I get kind of hysterical thinking of the boys in my class, most of them quite a bit smaller than I am and infinitely less mature, taking a girl out and all of a sudden getting passionate and everything.

It cracks me up.

"When's his birthday?" I asked.

"Oh, you and your signs of the zodiac," Jen sighed. "He was seventeen on April second."

"Oh, oh," I said. "Aries the Ram." I know a lot about Aries males because last year I was in love with Marlon Brando and he is an Aries so I found out all about the Aries male. I hasten to add that I am no longer in love with Marlon Brando. It was just a fleeting thing that came about when I happened to see an early movie of his on "The Late Show." I thought he was fantastic at the time.

"That means he is creative, a bad credit risk, and a natural rebel," I ticked off. "Also the Ram is unlikely to commit himself physically to more than one woman at a time."

"Well, gee, golly, that makes me feel better," Jen said. "For Gawd's sake, I went out with the guy once, I'm not engaged to him."

"Just thought you ought to know," I said. "Forewarned is forearmed."

"There you are." Nina came slinking onto the porch. "I've been looking all over for you, Niffy," and she looked at Jen and winked.

Just when Jen and I were getting to be friends again, Nina had to come along and spoil it.

"I have a couple of things I have to discuss with you, Niff," Nina said. "In private."

"I was just going," I said.

"Don't go on my account," Nina said in her absolutely stickiest voice.

"Gawd forbid," I said, smiling.

"Gawd forbid," I said again. It wasn't very good but it was the best I could do.

I heard them laughing in that awful way girls have when they have just said something very mean. I heard but I didn't turn around. I just went.

7.

I GOT on my bike and rode downtown. Most of the kids I know consider themselves too old and too sophisticated to still ride bikes, but I like to. There is a very free feeling, an abandonment, that comes when you whistle down a hill on a bike with your feet off the pedals. Especially if your brakes don't work.

I decided to go and see Carla McAllister. She works in Moody's bookstore on Main Street during the summers. She used to baby-sit for us a lot, for Nina and me and John, when she was just about the age I am now. She was the first baby-sitter we'd ever had who didn't treat us like fungus or turds or juvenile delinquents. I mean, she actually played games with us, read us stories, and let us put the ketchup bottle on the table, which is strictly against my mother's code of ethics. She also once drank some gin from my father's liquor closet because she had never tasted it and had always wanted to. I remember standing and watching her toss it down, gag, make a face, and spit the rest of it into the sink. Then she added some water to the bottle so they wouldn't know she had taken any. I thought that was pretty smart of her. My father complained for days that his martini tasted awfully weak. We never told, Nina and I. John couldn't talk at that time so he wasn't any problem. But we never breathed a word, which shows you how much we liked Carla.

Carla is a Capricorn. She was born the day after Christmas, which is a tough break. She's in college now, going into her third year. She is on a partial scholarship, as she is not only very pretty but exceptionally bright. I would say "brilliant," but that is a word that is so misused as a rule that I shy away from it.

Even when she was my age Carla was pretty, which is a rare thing. I read somewhere that there is nothing so ugly as a thirteen-year-old girl and I am inclined to agree. But when Carla was that age, she was already good-looking. Boys used to call her up when she was sitting with us and we would listen in on the extension. If the boys had ever known, what with some of the things they said, they would've killed us. Once in a while some of the creeps, the older ones, would drive up to our house and try to get Carla to let them in. She never would. She could've. Nina and I would've remained silent on that too, but she wouldn't. She has a great deal of integrity. Except for the gin bit — and everyone is entitled to a single lapse — she has the highest integrity.

She must have had a lot of boys try to make out with her but she also must have had a great supply of little jokes to leave them laughing and keep them from feeling rejected because they always came back for more.

Carla is not only pretty and smart, she is also kind and good and witty and wise. She is practically everything a person would want to be himself. She is close to perfect.

The only imperfect thing about her is her choice of a boyfriend. For months now, almost a year, she has been going steady with Dave Venon. Lots of people happen to think that Dave is the answer to a maiden's prayer. He is tall and handsome and has a cleft chin, which is considered the penultimate word among many of my acquaintances. He is smart. He also is very sincere. I mean, you can almost see the sincerity shining out of his eyes, which are blue. There is nothing wrong with being sincere. It is just that when a person creates an aura of sincerity around himself, it gets to be a drag. Mostly because people noted for their sincerity are basically humorless. That doesn't mean they may not laugh a lot. Dave laughs a lot. But basically, he is humorless.

Also, I think his mouth is weak.

I had found out through discreet inquiry that he and Carla were still seeing each other. I did not say much about him to Carla because if she liked him, I figured he must have hidden virtues.

Dave has been a lifeguard at our town beach for three years. He looks terrific in his pith helmet, and what with his physique and his tan and the whistle he wears around his neck to call back people who go out too far, I guess he is a sight to stir the corpuscles. He just doesn't stir mine, that's all.

I would like to add, and this is a sign of my spiteful nature, that in all the years he has been the lifeguard, he has not rescued a single person. He has not saved a single person from drowning. There was one near-drowning last year but that happened to occur on his day off. I know it is not nice of me to bring this up and it is also not his fault but I just thought I would mention it.

He gazes inscrutably over the horizon a lot, but he has never rescued a soul.

8.

THERE were a couple of customers in the store when I went in so I looked through some of the books on display. There is a great deal of trash being published these days but there is also a great deal of worthwhile stuff. I like the atmosphere of a bookstore. You figure that people there are interested in things of the mind rather than in clothes or cosmetics or other material things. I would like to work in one when I get old enough.

Carla rang up a sale on the cash register and then she came over to me and put her hands on my shoulders. I was pleased to note that we were almost exactly the same height.

"You are a sight for sore eyes, Tibb," she said. "Where have you been keeping yourself?"

"I've been around," I said. Carla is always glad to see me. That is another nice thing about her.

"How are your mother and father and John and Nina?" she asked. John has always been her favorite. John is that sort of person. He will go through life being people's favorite without even trying.

"They are fine, I guess. Nina is more of a pain than usual but that's par for the course. I have been feeling sort of down lately," I told her, "and, as a matter of fact, if it weren't for John, I think I would throw in the towel."

"Why? What's the matter?" Carla asked.

"Oh, everything and nothing," I said. "You know how it is."

Carla nodded. "It's your age. It's a tough one. I remember feeling the same way when I was your age."

I was shocked. "Not you, Carla. I remember you then. You knew what the score was. Boys were after you and everything."

"Let me tell you something," Carla said. "There isn't a kid alive who doesn't go through agony of some sort growing up. And don't you forget it. Not one kid alive. It's just the degree of agony, that's all. It always seems as if the other guy has all the breaks, but that just isn't so. I guess it's a necessary evil. You have to go through this travail to prepare you for life, to toughen you up. Hopefully, you'll be a better person for it. Your character is being strengthened by leaps and bounds."

"Oh, yeah?" I would have liked for her to go on talking, encouraging me. I liked the sound of her voice and the way she made me feel that I was a very important person. Then some old woman who must've had about a thousand grandchildren came in to buy books for them and she took out a list about a mile long and wanted Carla to give her a capsule comment on each book.

"I'll be over soon to see your family, Tibb," Carla said. "Give them my best."

I rode home and I felt very old and tired. Maybe because there's that big hill that was so much fun coming down. Going up it was almost more than I could handle.

A line from a poem by Christina Rossetti, who is practically my favorite poet although considered square by many people, if they've heard of her at all, goes: "Does the road wind uphill all the way? Yes, to the very end."

That was me in a nutshell. The road was going to be uphill right to the end. I got off and pushed my bike the last half of the way home.

9.

WHEN I got in, Nina was standing in the middle of the living room, her feet planted tragically.

"Mother," she said, "you'll never guess what's happened."

In addition to being an up-and-down-type personality, Nina is also, as are many Geminians, addicted to the drama. She says she would like to be an actress, but then I know so many girls her age who say the same thing that I do not think the world is big enough to handle all the would-be actresses.

"No," said my mother, "I can't guess. What has?" My mother sounded kind of weary. On occasions she has been heard to say that she is too young and/or too old to be a mother. I suppose that once in a while being a mother gets to be a drag. You have to realize that parents were once kids and were not always parents. It is hard, I admit, but it leads to a greater understanding of their problems if you can forget your own for the nonce. "Nonce" is another of my favorite words.

"I have been invited to a dance," Nina said, throwing her head back and stretching her neck. She has been stretching her neck for a couple of weeks now because she read an article about the desirability of having a swan neck and how you could make your neck longer by stretching it out every time you thought about it. It looks kind of peculiar but as long as she confines her exercises to the home, I guess it is all right.

"Oh," said my mother. "By whom?" She gets very grammatical in times of stress, I have noticed. Any other time she would have said, "Who by?"

"By Charlotte Forbes, that's who." Nina raised her voice. Charlotte Forbes is a pill in Nina's class at school. She is always talking about her clothes coming from Saks Fifth Avenue or one of those. As if anyone cared. I have even heard that Charlotte sews labels in her clothes that do not necessarily belong there. For instance, she took a label out of a blouse her rich

35

aunt sent her from a fancy shop and sewed it into a blouse she had bought in a discount house. That should give you a very clear picture of Charlotte Forbes.

"You and Charlotte should make a dandy couple," I said.

Nina gave me a look filled with such animosity that I was momentarily silenced.

"Explain," my mother said.

"Charlotte's mother is giving her a dance," Nina said.

"What for? So she can meet people?" I asked.

"Shut up!" Nina shouted.

"If you don't both behave you'll go to your rooms, big as you are," my mother said.

She meant it so I shut up.

"Charlotte's birthday is in two weeks and she's giving her a birthday dance and we're all supposed to bring dates."

The full horror of this struck both my mother and me at the same time. We sat silent. But it was not the end.

"And it is a formal. I will need a long dress," Nina said in almost a whisper.

"Charlotte's mother has social aspirations," my mother said after a bit.

"Charlotte's mother is absolutely the most terrific mother I have ever seen," Nina said. "I wish

I had a mother like Charlotte's mother. She is fluent in Spanish and she has four hairpieces."

There was nothing more to be said. My mother patted her home-grown, genuine hair which grew out of her scalp, and was still. I picked my toenails and wished I was someplace else.

"Will you ask Dad tonight? About the dress? I have to know by tonight. Everyone else is going and if I can't go, I'll die. I won't be able to face any of my friends. You never let me do anything."

I hope that when I am fifteen I will not turn out like Nina. I do not think I will but, on the other hand, you can never be sure of anything.

"Yes," said my mother, "I will ask him."

"Tonight? Promise? Tonight? I know what he'll say." Nina started to pace. "I know exactly what he'll say. He'll say we can't possibly afford a long dress. He'll say I'm still growing, I'm too young to go to a dance in a long dress, I won't be able to walk in one, I'm growing up too fast. Why do parents always think their daughters are growing up too fast? Do they want them to stay in diapers forever?" Nina started to cry. "I hate parents," she said. "I hate them."

"That is perfectly natural," I said. "Most kids hate their parents at one time or another. It is far better to let your hostility out than to keep it inside where it will only fester."

My mother started to laugh. Sort of hysterically but she was at least laughing.

Nina cried louder.

"Don't get yourself into a catatonic state," I said. "It's not worth it."

"You — " she said, clenching her fists. "You are such a slob I can hardly believe you are my sister. What did I do to deserve you? Why don't you run away from home and go live on a farm with the cows and horses? They wouldn't be able to tell you apart."

I happened to be smiling at myself in the mirror that morning, testing my personality quotient and also seeing how the new toothpaste was taking hold, when I thought I detected a certain resemblance between me and a horse. No special horse, just any one. Nothing you could put your finger on but, nevertheless, a resemblance.

Maybe Nina is more perceptive than I thought.

I pawed the ground with my feet and neighed. Jen and I used to practice neighing when we were small, and we were pretty good. We used to neigh happily and sadly and call to each other the way horses do. So now I neighed once or twice more. Nina started to cry again and my mother looked as if she had reached the end of her rope, a destination with which she is not unfamiliar.

"Go wash your face," she said, "and you'll feel better."

For some reason my mother thinks a clean face is a panacea for all ills.

"This is going to be a tough one," I said when Nina had gone.

"Yes," she said, sighing.

"Who do you think she will ask as her date?" I said.

My mother shuddered.

"At least I didn't ask her what boy she would take to the dance," I said. "You've got to give me some credit. I am not completely without tact."

"No," my mother said, "not completely."

10.

I COULD see that my mother was not going to bring up the subject of the long dress at the dinner table, which was just as well. Nina sat looking like a storm cloud with pink-rimmed eyes, sour as a kumquat. My father was tired and sort of withdrawn, as he frequently is when he comes home from work. He is a vice-president in an advertising agency. He is not *the* vice-president, just one of them, but it is still a pretty important job. However, what with the railroad, which often breaks down and makes him hours late, and the job, he is often somber when he gets home. It is a tough thing to be responsible for the food that our family eats, never mind the clothes our mother buys us. Even without long dresses.

My father makes fun of me for reading my horoscope all the time, but I remember when his said: "You may have been waiting for the sudden break which comes this week; something has to give."

That Friday he came home all smiles and said he'd been made a vice-president. I hastened to remind him of what his horoscope had forecast and that it was all written in his stars. I also hastened to say, "I told you so."

We cleared the table and Nina made faces at my mother and mouthed the word "Now" at her. My mother said, "Bring us some coffee in the living room, will you?" and Nina had that coffee going like a shot. She can move pretty fast when it behooves her.

In our house we have a telephone room under the stairs which is not too good for private conversations because there are so many cul-de-sacs surrounding it which are excellent for eavesdropping. But in this case, the telephone room was a boon. From it you could hear everything said in the living room.

"Nina has been invited to a dance," we heard my mother say.

"That so?" My father sounded sleepy. He probably wasn't really listening. He tunes himself out quite a bit. "A little young for that, isn't she?"

"She's been invited by Charolette Forbes. Her mother's giving her a dance. She has to have a long dress." My mother's voice was very calm, very matter-of-fact.

"A long dress!" my father said. "We can't afford it, can we? She won't be able to walk in a long dress."

"I think it will be all right," my mother said. "She can manage, and there's always Tibb. When Tibb needs a long dress, she can use it, so it's not such an extravagance."

Good grief! I got clutched up just thinking of me wearing a long dress. That would be the day.

But it seemed to satisfy my father. He said, "Well, if you think so," and then we heard the television, which meant the conversation was over.

We cleared out of there fast and Nina took the stairs ahead of me two at a time. My mother waited a few minutes and then she came up too.

"I talked to your father," I heard her say, "and he says you may have a long dress."

"Thank you, Mother," Nina said. From where I was in the hall, I could see her lying on her bed. "Thank you and Daddy for letting me go. There is just one thing I would like to know. I would like very much to know who you think I could possibly ask to go with me. Out of the huge group of boys I know, who can I ask?"

Oh, my Gawd!

"How about that nice Nelson boy?" my mother asked feebly.

A gurgling sound came from Nina's throat. My mother shrugged her shoulders. "I know of no one," she said.

I went into the bathroom to take a shower. But before I got into the tub, I had to remove John's troops. He never takes a bath without bringing all his little men, as he calls them, in with him. They are plastic soldiers, tanks, and boats enough to make the bathroom look like the Spanish Armada has just passed through. Then I turned the water on full force.

I heard the bathroom door open.

"Watch that shower curtain," my mother yelled. "Make sure it's inside the tub."

We have lost part of our kitchen ceiling several times due to leaking shower water.

"Mom," I said, putting my head out, "it's like the eye of the hurricane in here. It's great."

She smiled and closed the door. When I got out, she was standing on her head in her room. She has been taking a course in yoga at the Y but so far has only progressed to the point where she can stand on her head with her feet propped against the wall.

"Can't you do better than that?" I said. I stood on my head with absolutely no support at all. If I do say so, I am very good at standing on my head.

"That's wonderful," she said. "But then you're much younger than I am."

"What difference does that make?" I asked.

After some thought, she said, "I don't really know," and then she got down on the floor and tried again. She did much better this time.

When she was upright, I asked, "How did things go with Dad? About the dress?" which was hypocritical, seeing as how I already knew.

"Everything's fine," she said.

"Who's she going to ask?"

My mother put her hand to her forehead. "She doesn't know yet. She will think of some-one and when we have that problem settled, we will go to work on the dress. I anticipate more trouble with the dress than with the boy. Boys are a dime a dozen."

"That's what you think," I said, but I said it silently because I didn't want to stir things up any more than they were already.

11.

I KNOW you're not going to believe this but this is actually what happened.

The doorbell rang the next morning. Luckily Nina had just gone upstairs, her hair in rollers and some of yesterday's mascara smudged under her eyes. She looked sort of like a raccoon.

I went to answer it. A boy was standing there.

"Hi," he said. "Is Nina here? I was just passing by and I thought I'd see if she was home." He smiled at me and it occurred to me that he thought he was oozing charm. He was one of those charm oozers, a real phony.

Behind him, parked in our driveway, was a red convertible. Not brand-new, but shiny. Yeah, just passing by. I knew it was Tiger Jones. It had to be.

"Come on in," I said. "I'll get her. I'm Tibb. And this is John." John had egg on his face and his newest lanyard, which was purple and orange, around his neck. He put his hat on. That hat was a sort of security blanket for John. Then he stuck out his hand and said, "How do you do?"

He must've thought Tiger Jones was a grownup. John is very good about saying "How do you do?" to grownups. It always impresses them.

"Hey there, fella," the boy said. I didn't make that up, he really did say that. John backed off and pulled the hat down over his eyes. John has very good instincts for a boy of seven. He will go far.

"There's a boy downstairs," I said to Nina. She was standing in front of the mirror, sparkling at herself. This is when you smile a certain way, drawing your lips over your teeth, and if you do it right, you can make dimples. I have done this myself so I know. You can make dimples where there really are none, if you know how. Anyway, Nina's dimples disappeared and she said, "I don't have time for you this morning, little girl."

"O.K.," I said, "but there is. He came in a red convertible and he has 'Tiger' tattooed on his chest."

"I'll break your arm if you're lying," she said when she realized I wasn't.

One thing about Nina's and my relationship, we put it on the line.

Like a flash, she rearranged her face, took out her curlers, brushed her hair, put on her new blue jeans, a navy-blue body shirt, and some Blush on her cheeks. She was ready for anything.

"Well, hi," I heard her say from where I was listening at the top of the stairs. "What a nice surprise."

Who writes her dialogue, I wonder?

"Mom, this is Tiger Jones," Nina said. My mother was just coming home from the market, as usual.

"May I help you with those?" This Tiger really was suave. And he had to be at least sixteen, if he was driving. If he didn't have a tuxedo, he could always rent one. He was like a fly being drawn into a spider's web. He had shown up at a most fortuitous moment. One thing. Could he dance?

I went into the bathroom and ran the water until it was boiling hot. Then I filled the basin and put a towel over my head and steamed my face. This is sort of an instant sauna and it is very beneficial. It also shuts out the world. For the nonce.

When I got downstairs, Nina had gone. Tiger

had taken her for a ride. That's what *he* thought.

"Did she ask him?" I said.

"She is going to, I guess. I told her to be back by lunchtime. He seems like a nice boy, don't you think?"

"Mom," I said, "I'm the wrong person to ask. You know I can't face up to anyone who calls himself Tiger. I just can't."

I sat down at the kitchen table. "I saw Carla yesterday, and she said to tell you she's going to come over soon to see us all."

"That would be nice. I haven't seen her since Christmas. Is she still seeing that boy?"

"I guess so," I said.

"He certainly is handsome," my mother said.

"Yeah."

Then I heard the mail land on the floor in the hall. We have an old house with a mail slot to the left of the front door and you can always hear the envelopes slide through.

There was another post card from Susan Friend. This one was from Paris. It was a picture of the Eiffel Tower. It said: "Fab, fab, fab. Everyone speaks the most sensational French here. Even the tiny tots. See ya, Sue."

It was the only laugh I'd had that day and probably, the way things were shaping up, the only one I would have.

I figured if and when Sue got to Switzerland she would send me a picture of the Alps, telling me how fantastic it was that everyone there yodeled so well.

12.

IT just so happened that Tiger Jones was free the night of Charlotte's dance. Nina was on the telephone the entire afternoon, beating the drums, telling the tribesmen the news.

I wondered if Tiger had to go home and work his mother and father around the head and shoulders to get their permission to take the car that night, in addition to their paying for a rented tuxedo. Also did he have to tell them exactly when he'd be home?

My mother had to find out who was chaperoning the dance, what time it started, what time it was over, all like that. Nina said Well, if they didn't trust her, she could handle herself, and a whole bunch of other baloney which my mother ignored. She called Mrs. Forbes and, with the phony voice she uses on people she doesn't like, said she thought it was such a *lovely* idea, giving Charlotte a dance, and was there anything she could do, etc.

"They're having it catered," Nina said in an icy tone when my mother hung up. That was supposed to make mother feel like a peasant, but it is very hard to make my mother feel like a peasant. Like impossible.

"How swish," she said. "Tell me all about it. Don't miss a thing."

"Make sure it's chicken in the sandwiches, and not tuna fish, kiddo," I said. Nina threw her hairbrush at me but unfortunately it fell on the floor and the handle broke, so she had to borrow mine, which I graciously lent her with my sparkliest smile.

Then finally, when it looked as if Nina would have to go to the dance in her underwear, she and my mother settled on a dress they both liked. This may sound like a simple thing, but it was not. It was a large order. I have been shopping with Nina. I know. She always wants things that cost about double what my mother plans on spending and when she finds out she's going to have to settle on a little cut-rate number, she broods. She is a first-class brooder. The air around her sort of turns dark gray and although she does not stoop to weeping, there is a feeling of pent-up emotion that would knock you over. This attitude is quite infectious and puts the kibosh on any pleasure anyone might possibly get from a shopping expedition.

I myself am the type of shopper who goes into a store, tries on two garments, buys one, and leaves.

I imagine I am a salesgirl's dream. That's better than being nobody's.

Anyway, this dress was pretty. It was flowered linen and had ruffles around the neck and hem. It was very simple, which is what made it look expensive, my mother said. It *did* look expensive, and it also did things for Nina's figure, making her look svelte and curvaceous at the same time. That's a lot of things for $29.95.

Her friends started coming in, sort of like vassals coming in to see the liege lord, if you know what I mean. They stood around, humble in the face of magnificence, while Nina took the dress out and turned it this way and that. After much persuading she allowed herself to be coaxed into trying it on. That dress was tried on so many times I figured it would look as if it had come from a thrift shop by the time the dance rolled around. And if I was going to wear it when my day arrived, I would just as soon she quit trying it on. Naturally, I did not voice my thoughts.

The morning of the dance, I cleared out of the house. I wasn't up to the telephone calls, the discussions of how nervous Nina was, how adorable Tiger was, how sensational Charlotte and Charlotte's mother were. It was enough to make a person regurgitate.

I rode down to the bookstore. Carla was in the back room, eating her lunch. I told her about the dress and the dance and Tiger.

"Imagine Nina being old enough to go to a formal dance," Carla said. "It makes me feel old."

"Not as old as it makes me feel," I said.

"Next year it'll be you," she said.

"Yeah, and John'll be my date," I said. That made us both practically hysterical.

Then I said, "How's Dave?" I hoped she would say she didn't know, she wasn't seeing him any more. Instead she said, "He's fine," and offered me part of her Coke.

When her lunch hour was over, I left and rode down to the beach. It was cloudy so there weren't too many people there except for little kids whose mothers didn't know what else to do with them.

I went up to the lifeguard stand. Dave was

sitting there surrounded by a crowd of nubile creeps with too many teeth.

"Hi," I said.

"Hello there." He *was* good-looking, I had to admit.

"Save any lives lately?" I asked.

He looked puzzled. Then he laughed.

"Not today," he said.

I turned and walked away. The nubile creeps went on flashing their teeth. I didn't feel any better. Not any at all.

13.

TIGER had been sitting in our living room for more than twenty minutes, waiting for Nina. After my father had asked him about school and what he was doing this summer (he was going to summer school), my mother quizzed him on where he lived and how many brothers and sisters he had (he was an only child). Then John, who had spent the afternoon practicing, bounced a karate chop off Tiger's ear which had so much force behind it that Tiger's hairdo was disturbed and John knocked his own hat off. I figured I'd take up the reins.

"What sign are you?" I asked him.

His eyes became slightly glazed, and for all any of us knew, he was about to take it into his head to make a run for the door, and then Nina would make her entrance to no date. I wasn't up to the scene that would elicit so I tried again.

"What sign of the zodiac were you born under? When's your birthday?" I spoke slowly and enunciated every syllable so he would have no difficulty understanding me.

"Oh. Yeah. Well, like it's in a couple of weeks. It's the first of August."

"You've got to be kidding," I said.

"I wouldn't kid you." Tiger bared his fangs.

"That makes you a Leo then." I couldn't believe it. Somebody had goofed somewhere. This kid simply could *not* be a Leo.

"If you say so." What with Nina's and his dialogue combined, this evening promised to be one of the most sprightly on record.

Tiger was getting restless. He kept shooting his cuff to see what time it was. He had a corsage in a little box and he didn't know what to do with it. I offered to put it in the refrigerator. He said No, he'd hold it.

"I'm a Leo too," I said.

"Is that right?" He wasn't listening. What is there about me that always makes boys look at their watches, shoot their cuffs, and not listen when I talk to them? What is this strange power I wield?

Tiger looked at his watch again. Nina must

not have read about how you're supposed to be ready when your date gets to your house.

"It's the best sign in the zodiac," I told him.

He didn't answer. Nina entered on a cloud of my mother's Shalimar that made the eyes smart. Tiger knuckled *his* eyes for a couple of seconds and I thought it was the perfume until I realized it was his quaint way of indicating he thought she was gorgeous.

"Wow!" he said.

Nina smiled graciously. "Hi," she said. "Have you met my father?" which was pretty dumb considering my father had been caged with the kid for quite some time.

Then my mother came in and said "Please drive carefully" and "We'll wait up for you," both of which undoubtedly had Nina churning inside, but she was trapped with a male audience and all she could do was flash the ivories and press cheeks with my mother and father and also John, who was preparing another karate chop. My mother snatched him away just in time.

"Well," my father said when the car had pulled away.

"Well what?" my mother asked.

"How many years of this do you think you're up to?"

"This is just the beginning," she said. "First Nina, then Tibb."

"Not me. You'll never catch me going out with an ass like him," I said.

"Tibb!" my mother said. "Don't let me hear talk like that again."

"Well, he is one," I said.

"One what?" John asked.

No one answered.

"Tibb is right," John said. "He *is* an ass."

"John, it's bathtime." My mother took him by the hand and started up the stairs.

Just before my father turned on the television, John's voice came from the upstairs hall.

"What's an ass?" he asked.

14.

NINA'S and my bedroom is at the front of the house. I couldn't get to sleep. It was hot and I left the door open to let in a breeze. It must be very exciting to go to a dance in a long dress with a boy. Even a boy like Tiger. Let's face it, it must be very exciting, especially for the first time. Maybe it's more exciting the second and third times, though. Then you're more sure of yourself and are not suffering from a nervous stomach or problem perspiration or one of those.

Also you would know what to say, how to make small talk, how to make a boy feel you're interested in *him*. I have read plenty of articles telling girls what strategy to use to make boys like them. I have never read an article telling boys how to make girls like them. It makes me sore. How come they don't have to exert any effort? What's so special about the male sex that the female is always beating her brains out trying to get the fink to ask her out a second time? Suppose she had a lousy boring time the first date and she wouldn't go out with him a second time on a bet? Just suppose.

I find that thinking clearly this way is all very well when you are in bed in your own room. How it would work when you were actually out on a date is another matter entirely, of which I am aware. But it doesn't do any harm to think things through before you are faced with them in actuality.

I got up a couple of times and went to the window. Then I turned on the radio and listened to some music. The announcer said it was exactly twelve midnight. The witching hour. Nina's dance was over now. My mother had told her to come right home. They'd had a big argument over it. Nina had said maybe Tiger would want to go out for something to eat after. My mother had said she thought they were going to be eating practically the entire time they were at Charlotte's. Weren't they having a catered supper dance?

That wasn't the same thing, Nina had wailed. "I mean, out for a hamburger at the drive-in or something like that."

In her deadliest, most final tone, my mother had said Nina was to be in by twelve-thirty.

We shall see.

I must've dozed because the next thing I knew the radio said it was twelve forty-five. I got out of bed and went to the head of the stairs. She wasn't home yet. The lights were all on and the television was going and while I stood there, my mother came and looked out the front door.

"If she's not here by one, I'm going to call the police and see if there's been an accident," she said. She had already called Charlotte's and found out they'd left. My father came out and put his hand on her shoulder. "She's all right," he said. "Nothing could've happened." I went downstairs and sat in the living room very quietly so they wouldn't tell me to go back to bed.

At two minutes to one, the gravel in the driveway crunched violently. A car door slammed and I heard Nina racing up the steps. I guess old lover boy forgot his cool and wasn't seeing her to the door. The car pulled out of the driveway so fast it must've sprayed gravel all over the grass. My father would have a cow. He was always picking gravel out of the lawn mower.

"Where have you been?" my mother said. "I've been worried."

Nina got off one of her best wails. She wept and wailed and carried on so that I thought maybe she'd been raped. I have never known anyone who actually was raped but I've read plenty about it in the papers and have always been curious. I would like to question an actual participant as to the procedure.

"What happened? What happened to your dress? Come in and sit down." Nina tottered into the living room and lay down on the couch. She had aged about fifty years. It must've been some evening.

My father handed over his handkerchief and Nina really let loose. No one could understand a word she said. Finally my mother said, "If you're going to get hysterical, I'm going to call the doctor, I don't care how late it is. Try to calm yourself and tell us what happened."

"The little fink threw up all over my new dress," Nina said, loud and clear. "That's what happened. He threw up all over the front of my new dress," and then she started keening and practically beating her head against the wall.

"Maybe he was coming down with a virus," my mother said.

"That was no virus," Nina shouted. "The little fink was out in back of Charlotte's house drinking beer. That's what made him throw up. He was drinking beer like an alcoholic."

"Alcoholics don't drink beer," my father said. "How much beer did he have?"

"Did Charlotte's mother know about this?" my mother asked.

"Did he throw up while you were dancing?" I wanted to know. That would be kind of interesting, having your date barf all over you and also all over the dance floor. That would make it an occasion never to be forgotten.

"He didn't throw up until I punched him in the stomach," Nina said.

I forgot to mention that Nina is very strong. When we were little, she was such a good fighter all the other kids were afraid of her. She could and sometimes did lick any kid on the block, boys included. She had powerful arms and also plenty of muscles. It is only in recent years that she has decided to soft-pedal her muscles. I can understand this.

My father said, "Well, that's as good a reason as any to throw up, I guess. You punching him in the stomach. He has my sympathy."

"He had all this beer to drink and he was trying to make out with me in the car coming home and he put his arm around me and so I punched him."

Nina's eyes glittered, partly from tears, partly from rage.

My mother said, "I'm sure the cleaners can make the dress like new."

My father shook his head slowly.

"What do you know?" he said. "My little girl is able to take care of herself after all."

"They must've been some lousy jokes," I said.

"What jokes?" my mother and father asked.

"The jokes you have a stockpile of handy to keep the boy from feeling angry at being rejected," I explained.

"Oh, those," my father said weakly. My mother put her handkerchief over her mouth. Then Nina started to bawl again and my mother said she'd fix her a cup of tea.

My father sat there looking sort of dazed.

"Did any girl ever punch you in the stomach, Dad?" I asked him.

"Now that you mention it," he said, "I don't think any did. Blackened my eye once or twice and smacked me over the head with a pocketbook but punched me in the stomach, no."

"You weren't really trying, Dad," I said.

"I guess you're right. If I had it to do all over again, though, I can tell you this, I'd do better."

My mother called from upstairs.

"It's late. Come on up to bed, you two."

15.

JOHN has this way of waking me up which is
really unique. He stands beside my bed and
puts one finger, that's all, just one finger, lightly,
on my big toe or my arm and waits quietly until
I open my eyes.

When I woke up the morning after the dance,
John's finger was on my right ear.

I looked at Nina's bed. She was still asleep.
John does not wake Nina this way. He does not
wake Nina at all. He knows better.

He smiled at me. "Hello," he said.

I would have liked to go back to sleep for a
while but I told him I would get dressed and be
right down.

Only the top of Nina's head stuck out from under the blanket. Her hair looked sort of like a dandelion gone to seed. She had put some more streaking stuff on it and the sun had bleached it more and dried it out. She would have to put some mayonnaise on it to condition it. It is very good for the hair, even if sort of a disgusting idea.

John and I went through the refrigerator and got out some leftovers because Count was at our back door. Count lives next door. He is a Labrador retriever who is quite old but has a lot of dignity. He swims very well, even at his age. He is always hungry. I hope my mother didn't have any plans for those leftovers, as Count plainly enjoyed them. Then John put a lanyard around Count's neck and his hat on Count's head and we just sat there looking at the trees and not doing anything much. John and I are very peaceful together.

Unless he is trying out his karate chops, that is.

I heard someone moving around the kitchen. It was Nina, looking sorrowful and ancient. I felt sorry for her. I realized it had been a very long time since I had felt sorry for her. Since I had felt sorry for anyone but myself, if you want to know. It was sort of a nice feeling, to feel sorry for someone else.

She asked me if I wanted to split a bacon sandwich with her. I said Sure. My gosh, it had been ages since she had offered to split anything with me.

"The thing that gets me," she said suddenly, "was that I thought he was so nice. I didn't think I could be that wrong about a human being." Nina prides herself on being a very good judge of character. "It's a blow to my pride," she said.

I was going to say I thought he was an ass right from the beginning but the bacon started to burn and fat splattered all over the wall and by the time we got that cleaned up, I had decided not to say it, which was probably a wise decision.

"He said he was a Leo," I said. "I didn't believe him. Maybe he was left on somebody's doorstep and they just took a guess as to when he was born. I have never known a Leo who wasn't first-class."

"He looked so funny, though, when I socked him," Nina said. She was going to be telling this story a lot and she wanted to get it in shape. "I wish I'd had a camera. He looked so surprised!"

"It's probably the first time that ever happened to him," I said.

"And it may not be the last," Nina said darkly.

The telephone rang and I answered it. It was Jen.

"How was it?" she asked.

"How was what?"

"The dance, creepo. What'd you think?"

"Why don't you come over for a bacon sandwich? The chef is whipping one up."

Jen was there practically before I hung up. She only lives in the next block and she can really move when she wants to. She used to run the hundred-yard dash faster than any other kid in the school. She has very long legs.

So she sat down in the kitchen and Nina told her about the dance and what everyone wore and about the fantastic chignon Charlotte's mother had on and about Charlotte's dress that had been made for her and a bunch of other garbage.

I wondered how long it would take her to get to Tiger.

Finally Jen said, "What about Tiger? How did you two hit it off?"

Nina and I looked at each other and we started to laugh. We laughed so hard we were rolling on the floor. Jen sat there and looked annoyed.

"What's the joke?" she asked coldly. It is never fun to be left out of a joke. I know.

After a while we stopped laughing and Nina

told Jen what had happened. She laughed too, but then she said, "I don't think you needed to resort to violence," so Nina got mad and said he had it coming to him and then Jen left in a huff.

"Do you want my striped bell-bottoms?" Nina asked me. "I washed them and they shrank and they're too tight for me but I think they might fit you."

I said Sure, although I didn't really like them that much. But my gosh, I wouldn't have destroyed the atmosphere in our kitchen at that moment for anything in the world.

16.

THE truce was temporary.

The next day we were at each other's throats and Nina and Niffy were bosom buddies again. It had been fun while it lasted.

"I think I'll go down and see Carla," I said to my mother. "I haven't seen her all week. I love Carla, Mom. I really do. I wish she was my sister. She is a truly good person and you don't find too many of them lying around these days."

"Present company excepted, of course," my mother said.

I patted her on the head. "I like mothers who wear their own hair," I told her.

"That's too bad," she said, "because I'm seriously thinking of buying a wig. A very expensive wig."

"What color?"

"Red, I think. I've always wanted to be a redhead."

"Dad would have a conniption fit," I said. I had just been reading my horoscope for that day. It said: "Be sure to help good friends who are in trouble."

"Mom, your horoscope today is very apt," I said. "It says: 'Don't try to put new ideas into operation right now since they need more study before they can prove successful.' "

My mother said, "Do you suppose that means my wig?"

"I wouldn't be surprised," I said. "You better mull it over."

"Do you want anything downtown?" I asked her.

"No," she said, "but you could take a couple of books back to the library for me, if you will."

"Sure," I said. I liked the library. Especially in the summer when it wasn't filled with a whole mess of kids frantically doing term papers. I liked it best when there were just a lot of old ladies and men reading and also a lot of little kids who were so small they looked as if they couldn't possibly read. Once in a while you would even see a little kid sitting at one of the small tables reading away like mad, only if you looked closely you could see the kid was holding the book upside down. That always cracked me up.

"I want to come," John said.

Then I couldn't ride my bike. I'd have to walk.

"What'll you do downtown? It'll be pretty boring."

"I want to come anyway," he said.

Taurus the Bull.

Then Charlie D'Agostino came to the door. Charlie is a friend of John's whose mother is always trying to get rid of him. I can't blame her too much. Charlie is a devil. People in the neighborhood suspect that Charlie's mother drops him off outside houses and says, "Go visit so-and-so," and then drives off. Maybe.

"I'm here," Charlie announced.

"So I see," my mother said.

John and Charlie looked at each other and, without exchanging a word, they started their karate chops. My mother took each one by the arm and gently moved them out to the yard where they could chop away and not break up the furniture. They didn't even seem to notice the change.

"I hope they don't draw blood," she said. She had got very philosophical lately.

I got on my bike and was halfway downtown before I remembered I'd forgotten the library books. I decided I would take them next time. I felt like being alone all of a sudden.

17.

FAT chance.

The first person I saw when I stopped at the red light on Main Street was Jen. Wouldn't you know.

"Hey," she said, "guess who's getting married?"

"You," I said. "To Ernest Havemeyer."

Ernest Havemeyer is a very unfortunate boy we have gone through school with. He has everything wrong with him that he possibly could: bad breath, problem perspiration, dandruff; you name it, Ernest has it. I guess he doesn't watch the commercials on television much. Or if he does, he figures they're directed at the other guys. Even the hair tonic he uses is wrong. It smells like turpentine. Maybe it is.

"Ha ha," she said. "You're a riot. But really. Guess."

"Miss Nelson." Miss Nelson was our last year's English teacher. We had decided, Jen and I, that she was frigid.

"Carla McAllister, smarty. That's who," Jen said.

I tried to pretend that didn't shake me up.

"So what else is new?" I asked.

I had seen Carla last week. Last week she wasn't getting married. She would have told me. I know she would have.

"You didn't know Dave and she were getting married and you know you didn't," Jen said. "They weren't even engaged."

"Well, when you've gone steady as long as Carla and Dave have, it doesn't exactly come as any big surprise," I said.

"My mother ran into Mrs. McAllister this morning and she told her they decided on the spur of the moment. You know what that means."

I felt like smacking her.

"It doesn't mean anything except that they probably want to get married before they go back to college."

I remembered my horoscope for that day: "Be sure to help good friends who are in trouble."

"She won't be going back to college. Not in her condition," Jen said, smirking.

I would have hit her if we hadn't been standing on such a public corner.

"What's that mean?" I asked.

"Just exactly what you think it means. In the old days they used to call it a 'shotgun wedding.'" Jen smiled at me.

"You're a nasty, foul-mouthed, rotten little stink," I said. "To say things like that. Just because they decided to get married all of a sudden doesn't mean anything. You've been seeing too many dirty movies."

"O.K., wise guy." Jen's face was red. She didn't like being called "foul-mouthed." "You know all the answers. But it's true. You'll see. What's the big deal? Creep sakes, you act like Carla was some kind of saint or something. So she's pregnant and had to get married. So what?"

I turned and rode away from her. My heart felt as if it was going to pop right out of my chest and onto the pavement. I'd show her. I'd go right down to Moody's and talk to Carla and get it all straightened out.

Carla wasn't at Moody's.

"She's left us," the fat-faced, ugly female behind the counter said. "I understand she's getting married." The sunlight caught her eyeglasses and I could've sworn she was winking at me.

So then I rode my bike over to Carla's. I had started this and I was going to finish it.

I rang the bell and Carla answered. She looked pale, or maybe it was the dim light of the hall.

"Tibb," she said. "Come in."

"Hi, Carla. How's by you?"

Now that I was here, I didn't know what to say. I just stood there.

"Come on in," she said again.

"I can't," I said. "I have a lot of errands to do for my mother."

"I was going to call you," she said, "because I wanted you to know that Dave and I are getting married two weeks from Saturday. We want you and your family to come. It's going to be a small wedding. You'll get an invitation. Make sure John comes too. I specially want John to come."

"I don't know," I said. "I might be busy. I'll have to have my mother let you know."

"All right," she said, "but I hope you'll be there."

I looked at her through the screen door.

"What about college?" I asked. "Are you going to finish college?" I wanted to ask her, flat out. I wanted to say, "Carla, you don't *have* to get married, do you?" But I couldn't. I just couldn't.

"Eventually," she said, and then I knew that

what Jen had said was true. "We don't know where we'll be living or anything. We'll have to see."

I backed down the steps. I could hardly see, the sun was so bright.

"See you," I said. Carla did not smile.

I got on my bicycle and rode off. Then I came back. She was still standing there.

"Congratulations," I said.

"Thank you, Tibb," she said.

I was all the way home before I remembered you're supposed to congratulate the groom, not the bride.

I went to look at myself in the mirror. I am even uglier than usual because I have so many freckles. I always get freckles in the summer. Even on my knees. Nina gets a wonderful tan. She gets a little browner every day. She puts a gallon or two of oil on and then she starts turning like a chicken on a spit, my father says, and she just gets tanner and tanner.

I looked at myself a long time. I could not even cry.

18.

I'M not going," I said. "That's all there is to it."
We had got the invitation to Carla's wedding
in the morning mail.

My mother looked at me. "Why not?" she
asked.

"You know why not. I can't stand going to
weddings where the bride is pregnant."

"That's a nasty thing to say," my mother said.

"It's true, isn't it? I don't notice anyone deny-
ing it. Of all people, Carla, of all people. I can't
stand it. I absolutely can't stand it."

"Look," my mother said and she put her arm
around me. "I know how you feel. I know what
Carla has always meant to you. But you've got

to stop setting yourself up as a judge of others, Tibb, you really do. Just think of how she feels, and her parents. Think of them, not of yourself. And it isn't as if she and Dave weren't in love. They are, and they would have got married anyway. It's unfortunate that it had to happen this way."

"That's a masterpiece of understatement," I said. "I thought she was honest and good. And now she has to go and do this to me. She has betrayed me."

"No," my mother said. "She has betrayed herself. If anyone. She has betrayed herself and her family. They are the ones, not you. And it's not the end of the world, Tibb. I know it seems as if it is, but it's not. If Carla and Dave make a good life for themselves and their children and are useful, happy human beings, then they have accomplished a good deal. You must look at it that way."

"That's a lot of baloney," I said.

My mother took her arm away.

"How would you feel if it was me or Nina. What then?" I asked her.

"My heart would be broken," my mother said. "But I hope I would try to understand. I'm not sure that I would be able to, but I would try."

I knew she meant what she said. She would

try to understand if it happened to one of us. For some reason, that made me feel worse than before.

If such a thing was possible.

19.

I HAVE never been to a wedding," Jen said. "I
expect you'll have a terrific time. Everyone
says that weddings are the most fun."

I had decided to go. I had thought about it
after I went to bed last night and decided my
mother was right. I should not judge other people. Carla would feel bad if I didn't go. I knew
she would. Besides, my morning horoscope said:
"You can't escape the responsibilities you have.
Attend to them immediately or you may lose
out."

I figured that in a way, Carla was my respon-
sibility.

"What's so fun about weddings?" I asked Jen.

"Well, for one thing, there's pots of champagne and no one thinks anything of it if you get squiffy."

"Don't be asinine," I said. "That's the dumbest thing I ever heard of. Who wants to get squiffy anyhow?"

"Niffy does." Nina liked that. "Squiffy Niffy."

"Then, for another," Jen said, as if she hadn't heard, "you meet all kinds of people." She didn't like jokes made about her name. "And when I say 'people' you know what I mean, I trust?" She put on her inscrutable look, which only made her look as if she was going to burp. Jen is a very good burper. She can burp out something that sounds like "The Star-Spangled Banner" if you stretch your imagination a little.

"When you say 'people' in that soppy way, you mean boys."

"Well, after all, Dave goes to college and he's having some friends as ushers and all that. Dave is so good-looking," Nina cooed.

"If you like the type," I said coldly. "Dave's friends wouldn't give you the time of day. They're all as old as he is."

"Speak for yourself." Nina smiled smugly. "A boy in a car whistled at me yesterday and stopped and asked me if I wanted a ride and he must've been at least twenty."

"That's it," I said. "Start taking rides from

strangers in cars and you'll wind up sexually molested in a shallow grave."

"I didn't take the ride, finkhead. I just said he asked me."

"What'd you do, run into the bushes screaming?"

"Why don't you stop cutting everybody up into little pieces?" Jen said.

"I can't stand phonies." I got up and walked away. I would go to the wedding but that didn't mean I'd enjoy it.

Count was coming toward me across the grass and he had something in his mouth. He'd probably been raiding garbage cans for miles around. He has a bad reputation for raiding. He looked sheepish.

If a dog can look sheepish, can a sheep look doggish? Hey. Pretty good. I laughed. I enjoy my own jokes. If Jen had still been the good egg she used to be, I would have told her this one. It was her type. But now she was nothing but a colossal bore, what with her "boys, boys, boys" routine. And if it wasn't boys, it was "clothes, clothes, clothes." I don't see how we could ever have been best friends.

Count had a gigantic bone. It was so big it looked as if it had belonged to a dinosaur. He rolled his eyes around. I think he was afraid to put it down. Some other dog might take it away from him.

"You're a clod," I told him. He smiled at me. I swear he did. His mouth sort of stretched out on either side of the bone and he smiled. But he still didn't let go.

"You can't trust humans," I told him. "That's one thing about you. I can trust you to always be my friend. You're not going to get boy-crazy, like some people I could mention."

I sat down on our back steps and watched him and after a while Count let the bone drop and then he lay down and put one big paw on top of it and gnawed away.

John came out to empty our garbage. He is still young enough to consider this a big deal. He considers it a treat. He'll learn.

"Hey, John, I've got a good one for you," I said. He didn't have his hat on for once and his face was pale from being under the brim all summer. His arms and legs were very tan, though. He was two-toned.

"If a dog can look sheepish, can a sheep look doggish?"

I waited. Sometimes John is a little slow to get things. I think it is because I expect too much of him. He is only seven, after all, and maybe my humor is too sophisticated for him.

But then his face broke into wrinkles and he laughed the funny high laugh he has. I'm not absolutely sure he got it anyway, but he wouldn't let on. He has too much pride.

"I made it up," I said.

John nodded. "I thought so," he said.

"You're my favorite brother, kid," I told him.

He smiled. He is missing two front teeth. On him it is very becoming. We went inside and I lined the pail for him. He does not do such a hot job of lining garbage pails.

20.

TODAY is my birthday. I am fourteen years old. I got a card from Carla in the mail, which I thought very nice of her, considering her wedding is two days away.

My mother and father gave me a typewriter. That is what I wanted more than anything. My handwriting is execrable and this will help immeasurably. I am going to train myself in the touch system. I have already memorized the top row of keys and day by day I will memorize more until I have the whole keyboard in my head. Then I will tie a blindfold over my eyes and see how well I do. It should be an interesting experiment.

Nina gave me a pair of earrings which are

very nice. They are silver owls. I like them a lot. There is just one drawback. They are made for pierced ears. My ears are not pierced.

Hers are.

I have made it a rule never to let a cross word pass my lips on my natal day. I will stick to this rule.

Jen gave me a belt with a lion's head for a buckle, which I love. I also think it was nice of her, considering I have not called her "Niffy" once all summer.

My grandmother gave me a check for twenty-five dollars and a copy of *The Deerslayer* by James Fenimore Cooper. She said that I remind her of herself at my age. She was a romanticist too, she said, and James Fenimore Cooper was her favorite author.

I do not consider myself a romanticist but that is neither here nor there.

I have begun *The Deerslayer*. It is one of *The Leatherstocking Tales*, telling of life in early America. The leading character is a man named Natty Bumppo, who is noted for his honesty, probity, and integrity. I have not got very far along but already I feel rapport with him. He has also been pursued by quite a lot of girls, but he has never succumbed to the sins of the flesh.

John gave me a lanyard.

My mother asked me if I wanted a party. I

said no. I do not know who I would ask. I certainly would not ask boys, and most of my friends, except for Jen, are still away somewhere. That is the worst of having a birthday on August fifteenth.

I told her I would like to have just a small family party and maybe go to the movies afterward. If we could find a movie for family consumption, John could come along.

My horoscope for today is: "Just possible that from a distance or through professional channels your big break to travel or express talents comes again as in April."

Well.

In April I went on a trip to Washington, D.C., with my class and also in April I was in my class play. It was *Cheaper by the Dozen*, and I was one of the kids. I did not have a prominent role, only two lines, but still.

People who laugh at horoscopes should take another look.

21.

I WOKE up early this morning. It is Carla's wedding day. I had a dream last night. Carla was trapped in a well and was calling for help and I couldn't reach her. Then she was dressed up in a bride's dress and veil and walking down the aisle and when she got to the end there wasn't anyone waiting. At no time was there any sign of Dave.

Fortunately the sun is shining. It has been raining for almost a week and Mrs. McAllister must have been having a fit because they planned on having the reception outdoors and their living room isn't all that big.

We sent Carla and Dave some dessert plates.

Each one has a different flower in the center. They are very pretty. I picked them out.

I put some lemon juice on my freckles last night. I read somewhere that this would bleach them out. In the strong light of day it is obvious that this is a canard. I am going to wear a yellow dress I got for the dance after our graduation from eighth grade. It does not do much for me. Nothing does. I only wore it that once. The dance was one of those blasts where the girls stand around, the boys stand around, and only the clods who are going steady do any dancing. I do not know why I bothered going.

By next summer the yellow dress will be too small for me so I might as well wear it to the wedding.

No one will be looking at me anyway.

Nina is in another catatonic state because she has a big zit on her chin. She woke up this morning and there it was. She ate a fried Swiss-cheese sandwich and drank a bottle of soda for lunch yesterday because our mother wasn't home and she could have anything she wanted. That's why she got the zit. She is trying to cover it up with layers of cosmetics but it is still there. Serves her right.

John said he would not go to the wedding if he couldn't wear his hat. My mother is trying to find a tactful way to solve this problem. I say, give the hat to Count and he will eat it. I have never known him to turn anything down. Put a little A-1 Sauce on it and he'll never know the difference.

My father had made plans to play golf when my mother reminded him about the wedding. He stomped around for a while, muttering about how if it wasn't Carla, he'd go ahead with the golf. He has always liked Carla.

I am going to wear dark glasses. That way nobody can see my eyes and if you can't see a person's eyes, you can't possibly know what they are thinking. I do not want anyone to know what I am thinking.

22.

NINA popped her zit, my mother managed to hide John's hat where he can't find it, my father made another golf date for tomorrow, and my mother went to the hairdresser and came back looking very soignée indeed.

I am a dream in my yellow dress. It makes me look sort of jaundiced, like Mary in *The Secret Garden*. Or maybe it's a little leftover lemon juice on my patrician features.

At any event, we finally all got into our car and drove to the church. I wanted to sit in back but my mother whispered to the usher and he put us up front. The usher who ushed us was one of Dave's roommates at college. He was pretty nice-looking, if you go for the tall, athletic, broad-shouldered type. I myself prefer the intellectual ones. The ones with glasses and stooped shoulders which got that way because of the weight of the many books they have supported over the years.

Nina, of course, was practically swooning as the usher offered her his arm. I felt like giving her a good goose right then and there but figured that might be out of order.

I sat next to John. It was his first wedding too.

"Where's Carla?" he kept asking.

The music began. Heads began to turn and all the old ladies sighed and the feathers on their hats agitated and there was the maid of honor, who was a sex symbol if I ever saw one. She was practically popping out of her dress. Her name is Nancy Tyler. She was a friend of Carla's from high school. She was a nice girl and sometimes came over to our house while Carla was sitting with us.

"Hi, Nancy!" John called.

I put my hand over his mouth. "Hush," I told him. "You're not supposed to yell in church."

"Who's yelling?" he yelled.

Everyone looked at us. My mother moved away and pretended she was a total stranger.

Then came the bridesmaids, two of them. They were also sex symbols. They were nice-looking girls. I knew Carla would be next. I didn't turn my head. She had on a white dress and a white organdy kerchief tied under her chin. She was beautiful. She didn't look to the left or to the right.

Her father is considerably older than most fathers. He has white hair and carries himself very erect. I wondered what he was thinking about. I wondered if he wanted to punch Dave in the nose. Carla is his only child and he is very fond of her.

Dave stepped forth on schedule and he didn't forget the ring or anything. He and Carla didn't kiss after the ceremony. They came down the aisle and I will say this for Dave, he looked capable of taking care of her, if that's worth anything. He also looked very happy. Carla smiled at everybody. I don't think she saw any of us. John, for once, was struck dumb. He put his thumb in his mouth and looked like an idiot. Nina made eyes at the handsome usher, who was escorting Nancy Tyler down the aisle. Who did Nina think she was, competing against Nancy?

We all sort of milled around outside and then the bridal party got into cars and went off to the reception. Maybe I could sneak away and they'd never miss me. But then Mrs. McAllister, who was waiting for her husband, came up to me and hugged me. Mrs. McAllister also has white hair. They had Carla when they were pretty old.

"Tibb, darling, how nice to see you. And John and Nina." She smiled. "How good of you to come."

Carla used to take us over to her house some days and her mother would give us cookies and stuff she'd baked. If Mrs. McAllister wasn't whipping up dresses and skirts for Carla, she was baking. That was the kind of woman she was.

She acted as if this was just an ordinary wedding. She was doing what my mother would call "carrying it off beautifully."

"Carla looked lovely," my mother told her. "Perfectly lovely."

"Thank you. She did, didn't she?"

"Aren't you lucky? Such a glorious day!"

"What a lovely ceremony."

I guess people probably always say the same things at weddings.

Then Mrs. McAllister got into a car and everyone drove off to the reception.

We had to go through the receiving line, my mother said. We were supposed to say hello to everybody whether we knew them or not. I thought that was pretty dumb but it was one of the rules. Weddings are loaded with rules.

I shook hands with the bridesmaids and Nancy and then Dave.

"Congratulations," I said. I finally said it to the right person.

I thought he might be going to kiss me and I wasn't going to stand for that, so I stuck my hand out with a stiff arm and shook hands.

He looked different without his pith helmet.

"I'm glad you came, Tibb," he said.

"I hope you'll be very happy," I told Carla. I had my dark glasses on so she couldn't see what I was thinking.

"I already am," she said, smiling. "I really am. Hello, John."

She bent down and John shook hands with her.

"How do you do?" he said.

"That's Carla, you spaz," I whispered. I explained to Carla that I didn't think John knew her in those clothes.

He looked at her again. Then he took his hand away and planted a big kiss on her cheek.

"Hi," he said.

I think I saw tears in her eyes but there was such a bunch of people bearing down on us from the rear I couldn't be sure.

Like Jen had said, there were pots of champagne. I rather like it. I had one glass. Nina had at least two. There was a big wedding cake. We each got a piece of it to take home and put under our pillows. You are supposed to dream of the man you will marry if you sleep on the cake.

What a lot of baloney.

Finally Carla changed into her going-away costume and got ready to throw the bouquet. Nancy Tyler and the bridesmaids were standing directly below her, and there was a plethora of young men around who presumably would get ideas about weddings of their own.

Carla tossed her bouquet and there was a lot of jumping. I must've jumped higher than anyone else, because I caught it. As I said, I have grown almost three inches in the past year and I also am a forward on the basketball team. However, it was unpremeditated, I assure you.

Nina gave me a hard time going home.

"Of all the idiotic things I ever saw," she said. "You were practically the youngest girl there and you made a fool of yourself leaping up in the air."

"Knock it off," I told her. "If you weren't so dignified, you would have caught it yourself."

That is true. Nina is a much better basketball player than I am.

I put the cake under my pillow and I didn't dream at all.

That figures.

23.

NINA's nose has started to peel. I don't know why; she has never peeled before. The timing is bad because, on top of her nose peeling, she found out that there is going to be a dance at the canteen to which boys are supposed to ask dates. She found it out because bigmouth Charlotte Forbes called, in a turmoil. Two boys had asked her and she didn't know which to accept. What would Nina advise? Seeing as how this was the first Nina knew about the dance, due to the fact that not even one measly boy had asked her, things got tense.

After a gay chat of about half an hour, during which Nina managed to avoid telling Char that she had not been invited, Nina hung up. Then she started to brood.

I mean, I've seen her brood before, but this was something. Talk about air pollution.

"Gawd," she kept snarling out of the corner of her mouth, "will you look at me!" She blamed everything on her nose. She looked in the mirror about a thousand times, first at the right profile, then at the left, then full face. She had heard that actors and actresses have a good side and a bad and they prefer to be photographed, naturally, from the good. Nina had decided that her right side was better. She has developed a sort of lopsided walk from always trying to remember to approach the mirror from her right side.

My mother said, "Nina, would you please iron those few pillowcases and napkins I left in the basket?"

Nina put her hand to her head. "After I take a couple of aspirins," she said.

"Have you a headache?"

I think of my mother as a fairly perceptive woman but sometimes she draws a blank. Evidently she didn't see the gray cloud forming around Nina's head.

"Maybe you haven't noticed, but my nose is peeling," Nina said. "Maybe you don't know that my whole summer is ruined. I can't face my friends. I am a mess."

John came in to get some old frankfurters for Count. We usually have a supply of kind of stiff franks that have been pushed to the back of the refrigerator by mistake. Sometimes I think that John pushes them there. Count doesn't seem to mind that they are past their prime.

"What's the matter with your nose?" he asked Nina. That did it.

She went into a catatonic state. Keening like a banshee, if banshees keen, she raced out of the room.

"I'm not up to it today," my mother said.

"It's not only her nose, Mom," I said. "It's a dance at the canteen that Charlotte Forbes had two invitations to and Nina hasn't had one. That's all."

"That's enough." There are times when my mother feels like giving up. She says "I give up" quite frequently. I think this was one of the times.

"Things pile up at fifteen," she said.

"More than they do at fourteen?" I said. I hope not. They pile up plenty at my age. I don't think I can stand it if they keep on piling the older you get.

"Well, in a different way," she said. "It happens at all ages but somehow, at fifteen, you're not quite grown up but you're not a little girl any more, either. And you have moments of wanting to be both. It's a hard age."

"I don't look forward to it," I said. Which wasn't strictly true, only partly. Maybe things wouldn't pile up for me as much as they seemed to for Nina. We are not similar in personality, as I have mentioned.

Jen came to the back door. "Where's Nina?" she said. "I have something to discuss with her."

"She's upstairs," I said. "Her nose has started to peel and also she had a conversation with Charlotte Forbes."

"Oh," said Jen. "What did Charlotte have on her mind?"

"Oh, nothing was on her mind," I said. "She just couldn't decide whether to go to the canteen dance with Laurel or Hardy."

"Who's Laurel and who's Hardy?" Jen asked. She is a little dense sometimes.

I explained about Charlotte's two invitations against Nina's none, and about her peeling nose. Jen is fairly easygoing but even she got a little pale.

"Oh, my Gawd," she said.

Nina came into the kitchen. She had a big glob of some white stuff on her nose. Under ordinary circumstances, I would have said, "Who hit you with the pie?" or something equally clever. But I held my tongue. I have always liked that expression. Have you ever tried to hold your tongue? It is very slippery.

"Come on over to my house," Jen said. "I've got a fantastic new record."

"I look so ghastly," Nina moaned. "I feel so ghastly."

I was going to suggest that she borrow John's hat but I didn't. She went anyway. Probably they took the back way through the garbage pails so no one would see them.

I didn't go. Instead I stayed at home and did something I have never done before. I got out the laundry basket and did the ironing that Mom had left for Nina. I actually did. Every time I think of it I am impressed. I never even said I'd done it. I never even got credit. It was my *beau geste*. I just took the pillowcases to the linen closet and put the napkins in the drawer, and I didn't say a word.

Nina didn't thank me, either. But that was all right. She was in such a state when my mother asked her she probably didn't remember she was supposed to iron.

24.

I THINK I have changed a lot this summer. I have grown and matured and I am also a sadder and wiser person. This comes with age. My character is being strengthened by leaps and bounds, as Carla said.

I know that people and things are not always what they seem. I know that people you think are strong are sometimes weak. I know that the first date in a long dress can turn out to be a bomb. I know that I am not as nice as I thought I was. I have always thought of myself as a fairly nice person. But when the chips were down, I turned out to be mean and small and almost didn't go to Carla's wedding.

I hope I have learned not to sit in judgment

on people. I hope I have learned not to think I am always right and the other guy is always wrong. I hope I have learned to take a broader view of the world. As long as my standards remain mine and I stick to them, then it shouldn't matter what other people's standards are.

I hope I have learned not to contemplate my navel as much as in the past.

I have finished reading *The Deerslayer*. I am in love with Natty Bumppo. He was nothing but good. He was kind, noble, soft-spoken, honest, and all good things.

I intend to make a study of him. I would not be in the least surprised to find that Natty Bumppo was a Leo.

My horoscope for today says: "Hope begins to make you optimistic. Your mind will expand now. New ideas bring exciting possibilities."

I hope this is prophetic.